Tall
Inside

For Stephanie and Sidonie, Mary's twins,
who will always be small.
    JR

For MJB
    AE

Text copyright © 1988 Jean Richardson
Illustrations copyright © 1988 Alice Englander
First American edition 1988 All rights reserved.
This book, or parts thereof, may not be reproduced
in any form without permission from the publishers.
First published by Methuen Children's Books Ltd,
London, England.
Printed in Italy.
First impression.

Library of Congress Cataloging-in-Publication Data
Richardson, Jean.   Tall inside.
Summary: Short Joanne is unhappy with her size until she
meets a clown who reminds her that being tall on the
inside is more important than being tall on the outside.
[1. Size—Fiction.   2. Clowns—Fiction]
I. Englander, Alice.   II. Title.
PZ7.R39485Tal   1988   [E]   87-19096
ISBN 0-399-21486-0

Jean Richardson and Alice Englander

Tall Inside

G. P. Putnam's Sons   New York

J oanne was small for her age.
When they stood in line at school,
she was the shortest person in her class.
    "You'll catch up one of these days,"
her mother said, as if it didn't matter.

"All the best things come in small packages,"
her father said, giving her a kiss.

"You could try eating rubber bands. Then you
might stretch," her brother Matt said.

They just didn't understand.

Most days Jo went next door to play with her best friend
Jenny. They had just learned how to do handstands and
spent hours in the garden practising.

One day Jenny's cousins Rosie and Ann joined them.

"Let's start a club," said Rosie, who couldn't
do handstands. "To join you have to pass a test.
Everyone has to jump up and swing from
that branch."

Rosie did it easily, because she was tall.
Jenny and Ann just made it. Jo couldn't reach at all.

"You can't join," Rosie told her. "You're too short."

"I don't want to join your silly club anyway," said Jo.
And ran off home.

But she did. She went up to her bedroom
and told her bear, Humpty. Tears splashed on to him,
but he was used to getting wet.

   "Anyone want to come shopping with me?"
her father called up the stairs.

   "Yes," said Jo, quickly drying her eyes on Humpty.

On the way home they saw a ring of people
laughing and clapping at something.
 "What's going on?" Jo asked.
"Oh please, let's find out."
    Her father could see over the heads of the crowd,
but Jo had to wriggle her way to the front.

The first thing Jo saw was a pair of striped
trouser-legs that seemed to go right up
into the sky. Miles up was a clown face
with a cherry nose and a huge smile.
He was the tallest man Jo had ever seen.

A small man was trying to give the clown a message.
 "Hey, Lofty!" he shouted, but Lofty didn't hear him.
He waved his handkerchief, but Lofty didn't see him.
Finally he began juggling with coloured balls.

Lofty tried
to catch them
but he wasn't
quick enough.
   "Come and help
me," he called
to the crowd.
"Who's good at
catching things?"

"Me! Me!" several children shouted, and Lofty invited them to join him in the ring.

"Me! Me!" Jo shouted, but Lofty didn't see her.

She was too small.

"Me! Me!" she shouted again, but her voice only reached to Lofty's waist.

He turned away, but Jo wouldn't give up. She ran after him and tugged at his trousers. The crowd laughed.

"What have we here?" Lofty said, peering down.

"Please can I help?" It was Jo's biggest voice, and it made her cheeks as red as Lofty's nose.

"Shall we let her help?"
Lofty asked,
and the crowd
roared "Yes."

The children followed Lofty to a van where they climbed in and found a pile of clown costumes. Jo wanted the red one with black pompoms, and pulled it away from another girl.

A girl with spiky blue hair was in charge of makeup.
She rubbed white greasepaint on Jo's face and
ringed her eyes with black circles.
Then she drew her a big
upturned mouth.

One boy had a clown wig
with hair sprouting from
a bald patch. Jo wore
a red nose like Lofty's.

A clown showed them how to do somersaults on a big mat,
and they all rolled over – and over. A boy did cartwheels
and Jo did her handstand – and stayed up for ages.
The crowd clapped.

Then they paraded round the ring, copying the clown's
funny walk. Jo waved to her father.

Then she waved to Lofty,
and he threw her a squeaker
that made a rude noise.

When the show was over,
Jo didn't want to take off
her clown outfit.
She shook her head
when the makeup girl
offered to clean her face.
   The girl smiled.
"Do you want to keep
the red nose?" she asked.
Jo nodded. "OK. It's yours."

Jo looked at her spiky
blue hair and thought
she was the luckiest
person in the world.
Imagine being a clown
every day!

Suddenly Lofty put his head
round the door of the van.
He was much too tall to
climb inside. One minute
he towered above Jo.
The next he hopped into
the van and was sitting
beside her. Jo couldn't
believe it.

Then she saw a pair of legs
in long striped trousers
leaning against the side
of the van.

Lofty smiled. "You didn't think my legs were that long, did you?"

"Well..." Jo didn't want to admit she had. "It must be wonderful to be so tall," she said. "Especially when you're small like me."

Lofty measured her with his eyes. "When you've finished growing," he said, "I reckon you'll be looking down on me."

"But don't you mind being short? I do."

Lofty's eyes twinkled. "The way I look at it," he said, "I don't mind being small because I can make people laugh. And that makes me feel tall inside."

Over supper that night Jo and her father
told her mother and Matt all about the clowns
and about how good Jo had been.

Matt was jealous. He wanted to try on
the red nose, but Jo wouldn't take it off.

"You'll have to take your makeup off before you go to bed," her mother said. "You can't be a clown forever, darling."

She gave Jo a cleanser and some tissues.

Jo looked at her clown face in the mirror for the last time. She felt she was saying goodbye to the clowns.

First she wiped off her great big eyes.
Then she wiped off her bright red cheeks.

And finally she wiped off
her great big mouth.

But she took the red nose
and put it under her pillow.
   Wait till I tell Jenny,
she thought. And she fell asleep smiling.